DOUBLE CROSS

The Trigger

BUTTERS PI

RORI BLEU

ROSIE CHAPEL

First printing: 2025
ISBN: 978-1-7637753-8-1 (ebook)
ISBN: 978-1-7637753-9-8 (paperback)

Ulfire Pty. Ltd.
P.O. Box 1481
South Perth
WA 6951
Australia

Cover Design: Rebecca Norman
Images Courtesy: Canva and Deposit Photos
Designed in Canva using appropriate licences.

❀ Formatted with Vellum

DOUBLE CROSS

Butters P.I.

*"Down these mean streets a man must go who is not himself mean,
who is neither tarnished nor afraid.
The detective must be a complete man and a common man and yet
an unusual man.
He must be, to use a rather weathered phrase, a man of honor—by
instinct, by inevitability, without thought of it, and certainly
without saying it.
He must be the best man in his world and a good enough man for
any world."*

The Simple Art of Murder
Raymond Chandler

CHAPTER ONE

1938 - San Francisco

Friday March 18th, 1938, began as yet another dreary day in San Francisco. Whoever was in charge of the waterworks upstairs had refused to turn them off for the past couple of weeks, and I would not be at all surprised if people started sporting webbed feet.

That was the least of our worries, given that far beyond our safe but, currently, very damp metropolis, the drums of war were beating loudly.

Francisco, no relation to our City by the Bay, Franco and his Nationalist troops were in the midst of battling the Republican government for control of Spain.

Hitler had just annexed Austria and turned his attention to parts of Czechoslovakia. *I guess he figures Germany rules over Germans no matter where they live.*

The Italians, under Mussolini, continued rattling their

sabers against the woefully under armed Ethiopian Forces in east Africa.

Meanwhile, Hirohito's Japanese Imperial Army was in the midst of massacring thousands of peasants in China.

From a relatively objective viewpoint, it appeared half the planet had crossed the threshold into senseless bloodshed, for the sake of patriotism, despite England, France, and the good ol' US of A continuing to preach peace.

While the rest of the world was going to hell, yours truly made my way to Aunt Clara's Diner for breakfast. Two eggs, bacon, toast… lightly toasted and buttered… and coffee. It was a standing order which Clara had ready to go Monday through Friday at 7a.m., sharp.

As a member of San Francisco's finest, having breakfast waiting meant I would not be late for work. The captain abhorred tardiness and chewed my ear off whenever I missed roll call.

I was stabbing my eggs with a fork when I saw a slender hand reach for my fedora and lift it from the counter.

I caught a whiff of cheap perfume as the shapely woman sitting on the stool next to me leaned against the red, Formica countertop.

Out of the corner of my eye, I caught sight of a pair of legs which went on for days, one draped over the other. My hat, perched on her head at a cocky angle, hid one eye.

I doubted my current lady-friend would be happy with some other woman's scent on any part of my suit.

Oh well, she was fun while it lasted.

"As I live and breathe, if it isn't my favorite police *dick*, Sergeant Jacob Butterfield." My unexpected breakfast guest cooed. Her Brooklyn accent, obvious.

"Morning, Mae, and watch your mouth, otherwise I'll have to run ya in for lewd and lascivious behavior." I recognized the voice and continued spearing my eggs.

This elicited a throaty laugh. Mae removed my hat, fanned herself, and replaced it. "To think I would be accused of being lewd with a member of San Francisco's Vice Squad."

Around my food, I reminded her, "You forget, I've been promoted to Homicide. Besides, you and your roommate have been through most of the City Council, so I doubt hitting on a cop would be too much of a stretch." Adding, "By the way, where *is* your partner in crime? I thought the two of you were joined at the hip."

"Junie? She's got her nose glued to The Emporium's front window, gawking at a dress she can't afford. I swear to God, you'd think she was a kid at Christmas."

Mae Oliver and June Davies… who never did 'fess up as to whether their names were aliases… were part of my first, second, and third arrests after I joined the Vice Squad. The pair were taxi-dancers at the Hippodrome… the Barbary Coast dance club where anything, including dancing, took place on the floor between the girls and the male customers.

The pair also shared a room in a flophouse in the Tenderloin District of the city. From time to time, they supplemented their income by turning tricks out of their place.

I had made it a habit to cruise by on those nights, just to check on them. If both shades facing the street were up, it was their way of signaling they had a *guest* who was not playing nice.

This prompted me to pay them a visit, have the lot arrested, and send them to Central Booking. The girls got a meal, spent the night there, and I ensured they were bailed out the next morning.

The arrangement was mutually beneficial.

In exchange for my watchful eye, they kept me abreast of the goings on in the Red Light and surrounding districts.

Spinning around on the stool, Mae helped herself to my toast and coffee.

I groused, "Please, help yourself. I didn't need my morning Joe."

At that moment, I heard the stool on the other side of me scrape the floor and saw an equally slender hand help itself to my bacon, while its accompanying voice complained, "Twenty dollars for Chrissakes. Can you believe they want twenty dollars for that dress? Who do they think they are, Saks Fifth Avenue?"

"I told you it wasn't worth it," Mae said across me.

"But it's so cute," June whined. "If that wasn't bad enough, some old witch in the store came out and shooed me away. I mean I have money."

"Really? How 'bout coughin' up your part of the rent then?" Mae huffed.

"I said I had money. Didn't say how much." June smiled sweetly at her roommate.

Getting a word in edgewise, I greeted the new arrival, "Morning, June. Didn't lockup have anything for breakfast this morning?"

June was the shorter and curvier of the two. At first glance, fresh faced and dewey-eyed, she looked much younger than Mae, but, if you took the time to take a second, you saw a different story. One of a hard life on the streets, and of experiencing more than any woman should.

"Oatmeal," she exclaimed. "How does the city expect a poor girl to survive on oatmeal, and not even any toast." My second slice vanished from my plate.

"Clara," I bellowed. "Can you get these two moochers breakfast for me?"

"On your ticket?"

I nodded, snatching my coffee cup from Mae to have Clara refill it.

Clara rolled her eyes. She did not appreciate having women of ill-repute in her establishment, and made no bones about it. Inevitably, however, her desire to make a profit always outweighed her moral compass.

"Comin' right up, Sergeant."

While the ladies raided my plate, awaiting their own meals, I decided to get to the bottom of their sudden appearance.

"While your company never fails to cheer me up, besides eating on my dime, to what do I owe the pleasure of this visit?"

The women stopped munching on my breakfast and glanced at each other nervously. They looked around, then Mae leaned close.

"We thought you might be..." Their food was served, and she paused, waiting for the older woman to leave, and curling her lip when Clara did not move fast enough for Mae's liking.

Once the owner had disappeared into the kitchen, Mae continued, "...interested. The boss said there are some heavy hitters from New York coming to town and he wants a bunch of us girls on hand to *entertain* them."

"Any idea who they are and what's going on?"

It was June who answered, "No, but Gus..." her afore-mentioned 'boss', "...was not his usual jolly self when he told us about the extra hours. Truth be told, he looked terrified. I heard him talking to his brother—"

"You mean eavesdropping," Mae chided, digging into her meal, after leaving me with just my coffee.

"Potato Potahto," June flung back chirpily, quoting a phrase she had adopted from the recent movie, Shall We Dance, and used at every opportunity. "Be that as it may, it's not just the gentlemen from New York, but also some of the commissioners on the city planning board."

"Planning board?" I queried. "Why?"

"How should I know?" June snapped back. "Isn't it your job to find out?"

Acknowledging this was all I was going to get from the pair, I snatched my hat from Mae's head, tossed two bucks on the counter, which covered everybody's breakfast, and assured the tip was adequate enough for Aunt Clara to continue to treat me as her favorite nephew.

I dipped my Fedora to the women on the stools, "I bid you good day. Oh, and June, that rolling pile of junk you drive—"

"Don't be cruel, my Maxwell is a classic."

"Right… maybe a classic joke on the Jack Benny Show," I derided the 1919 jalopy, which was usually broken down in front of their place. "It's getting a ticket for blocking a hydrant."

"Shit," was all she cried, and scarpered, trying to chase down the traffic cop who had written the ticket.

I chuckled and followed her out, making my way to the SFPD's Southern Station, and the Homicide Department.

CHAPTER TWO

While San Francisco's reputation during the gold rush was that of a wild and lawless city, the criminal activities perpetrated in the late twenties and thirties made those days look like a picnic in the park.

Our fair city had survived a gang war, which began in 1928 with the murder of bootlegger, Jerry Feri, and led to a trail of bodies of those trying to control the Waterfront and the lucrative drug trade coming from Asia.

The murders, and the war itself, ended back in '32, with the death of one Luigi Malvese. The hijacker, bootlegger, and gunrunner turned racketeer was gunned down in broad daylight as he strolled through a supposedly friendly neighborhood.

With the competition conveniently disposed of, Francesco "Frank" Lanza stepped in to fill the void to consolidate the various criminal enterprises under a single family — his.

Any missteps by their underlings were met with swift retribution, usually, in the form of a bullet to the head.

Lanza always covered his tracks. He portrayed himself as

a legitimate operator, establishing the newest tourist trap, Fisherman's Wharf, and opening a restaurant there with his business partner, Giuseppe Alioto.

When Lanza died of natural causes in 1937, Anthony Lima, a violent and unstable gangster, assumed authority because Lanza's son, Jimmy, was deemed too young for the responsibility.

If what Mae and June had told me was true, the Wild West was about to explode again in a much bigger war between the two coasts, with the potential, like the ridiculous alliances which led to the Great War, to spread the violence across the entire country.

Settling behind my desk, I lit a cigarette, and took a deep drag, spotting my partner, Lieutenant Louis Mazzetti, engrossed in a report.

"Whatcha got there, Lou?"

"Oh, morning, Jake. Glad to see you managed to make it in before the end of the shift."

"Very funny," I shot back.

"Good thing O'Connor wasn't looking for you."

"Okay, okay, point taken. Now, what are you reading?"

"Another shooting in Chinatown, off Sacramento. The squad found two guys in a car. Looks like they were ambushed. Dead before they knew what hit them."

"Why do you think that?"

"The .45s they were packing were still holstered."

"Were the vics Orientals?" I asked.

"Nope," Lou answered, still reading, "two white guys in a fancy Caddy. Looks like the Tongs are getting a little overprotective of their territory, 'cuz the triggerman wanted to make a messy statement. Sprayed lead all over the car."

"Makes sense, considering what my sources—"

"You mean Mae and June." Mazzetti shook his head. He did not put much credence in information provided by prostitutes. He considered it nothing more than pillow talk from their customers to make the latter seem more important than they really were.

"As I was saying… my sources told me, there's some big-time wise guys comin' in from the Big Apple for a meeting with the locals. I'm guessin' it's a takeover. We could be looking at a territory war getting ready to reignite."

"Think we should get in touch with the Feds?" Lou's question took me by surprise.

"What for? I'm sure we can handle whatever comes up."

"To keep our hands clean," he replied in a hushed tone as he skirted my desk on the way out of the office door.

That confused me… *clean from what?*

His, "I'm going to the bakery, I'll grab you a donut and meet you at the car," prevented me from questioning him further.

"Car? Where we headed?"

"Chinatown… where else?"

The word *tong,* meaning gathering place, refers to secret societies set up by the Chinese in the US, purportedly, to protect their fellow immigrants. It did not take long for these same power-hungry organizations to become ruthless gangs who subjugated the very people they were supposed to help.

They forced women into prostitution or trafficked them

across the Pacific and kept a close eye on the distribution of opium and cocaine throughout the Chinese communities.

Rumor had it, one man oversaw all of the activities — a certain Zheng Wei who claimed to be a descendent of the infamous pirate couple Zheng Yi and his wife, Ching Shih. The latter had, upon the untimely death of her husband, assumed sovereignty over a fleet of fifteen hundred ships and eighty thousand men, controlling all shipping in the South China Sea in the early years of the nineteenth century.

The only force able to defeat her was time.

She grew tired of the life as the most successful female pirate in history and persuaded the Chinese emperor to grant her a pardon, allowing her to retire as a respected member of Chinese society.

The same thing could not be said for the rest of the Zheng clan. Subsequent generations continued to prey on Asian shipping, right down to the present head of the family, the wizened gentleman sitting across from us, sipping tea.

Setting his cup down with both hands, the man accorded us a skeptical look. "Tell me, gentlemen, what brings San Francisco homicide to my humble abode?"

It was Mazzetti who replied, "I am sure you are aware of the murder which occurred on your turf this morning. We are—"

"Lieutenant Mazzetti, I have no idea why you refer to Chinatown as *my turf*? Are you insinuating that I operate a nefarious enterprise from my shop? As you can see, I am but a simple importer of Chinese herbal medicine and teas."

To anyone of a less sceptical mind, this was true. Zheng's shelves were stocked with assorted boxes and pouches labelled in Chinese script, all of which could mean *Opium*, and we would be none the wiser. Neither was there any point in me voicing my suspicions. Zheng's business practices were not the reason for our visit, and he was a past master at obfuscation.

"Regrettably for those two gentlemen, it was a case of being in the wrong place at the wrong time." Zheng's sorrowful expression did not fool me for a second. "Strangers are not welcome in the Chinese District in the early morning hours. They were probably mistaken as a couple of those gangsters your, oh so diligent, force seems unable to rein in."

"Are you admitting your men were involved?" I countered, reading between the lines.

"No, no, Sergeant Butterfield, quite the contrary. My employees are law-abiding citizens and, on the subject of the law, why are two homicide detectives from the Southern Station investigating a crime which falls under the jurisdiction of the Chinatown Squad?"

"It's an ongoing enqui—" Mazzetti started to explain, but Zheng cut him off.

"No, Detective Mazzetti, the two of you viewed this as an opportunity to shake down a poor *Chinaman*." The tone in Zheng's voice left us in no doubt he considered the term an age-old slur used by whites against his people. "Just because you may have heard I am generous to the local police squad's benevolence fund..." it was no secret among the SFPD that corruption and grift was rife in the Chinatown Squad. "...does not mean my generosity is limitless.

"That said," his expression turned sly, "if you require financial assistance, you only need ask. I am prepared to extend my charity to a couple of homicide cops."

I glanced at Lou, whose face had turned a shade of red, of which a tomato would be envious. Before my partner had a brain aneurysm, I interposed, "You have misunderstood our visit, and had I half the inclination, I'd run you in for trying to bribe us."

Zheng feigned shock at the accusation, but we knew it was a ploy.

"With that, Mr. Zheng, we bid you good day, but…"

"But what?" Zheng's annoyance was betrayed by the hint of a long suppressed Cantonese accent.

"Do not think this is our last visit."

Zheng's attitude shifted, and an odd smile tilted his thin lips. "Then, allow me to offer some information for free. A large occidental…" their equally distasteful word for us… "was seen creeping around Chinatown."

"Do you have a description?" I asked, June's remark about Gus being scared coming back to me

"Big and white, but then, you all look the same to us," he replied snidely. "One last piece of advice, Detective Butterfield, if you are determined to make your presence known in Chinatown again, understand you do so at your own risk. As you have seen, these streets can be dangerous at night."

"Surely, you didn't just threaten an officer of the law?" I growled at him.

"I would never think to do so. Consider it friendly Daoist enlightenment."

CHAPTER THREE

It was past noon by the time we left Zheng's office.

"You hungry?" I asked Mazzetti.

"As much as I'd like to fleece you for lunch, I've got a couple of places I have to stop at first," he replied.

"I ain't got anything on my calendar for the rest of the day. I can tag along if you want."

At that, a queer look descended over Mazzetti's features, along with a nervous twitch like a kid caught lying to his parents. "No, it's okay. Just need to pick some stuff up for the wife."

"Georgina not feeling well?" I pressed, to see whether that rattled my partner.

"Y-Ya know, women's stuff," was all he said, as though that was enough to satisfy my curiosity.

My suspicions deepened. Lou was the last man on earth willing to scour the store for anything like that, wife or not.

Was my partner cheating on his wife of twelve years?

God knows I was not one to preach, but I'm a single guy, and even then, I don't play around. Lou and Georgie were different from many law-enforcement couples who couldn't deal with the stresses of the job. They had been together for years, and their marriage seemed inviolable, impervious to outside interference. That he might be stepping out bothered me, but I held my tongue.

"Tell ya what," Lou suggested with a half-cocked grin, "I'll drop you off at the office, and meet ya for breakfast at Clara's place on Monday.

"You're not going back to the office later?"

"Nah, I told the captain I was taking the rest of the day off."

"Okay," I said with a shrug.

Louis Mazzetti was not about to get off the hook that easily.

Mazzetti pulled into the spot reserved for our unmarked car. Alighting, he headed to his two-toned Oldsmobile L-Series sedan, shouting a farewell over his shoulder.

I wasted no time jumping into my 1932 Burgundy DeSoto Six... yes, it is my pride and joy... and gave him enough of a head start that he would not notice me.

I followed him toward Chinatown, which led me to believe he had some unfinished business with Zheng. I hoped it was to give the shady proprietor an earful for insinuating we could be bought.

Instead of turning into the ornate neighborhood, he continued on to Pacific Street, and the even seedier side of the city.

Mazzetti parked the large automobile at the end of the street where the strip clubs began. I snagged a spot a block behind him.

From where I sat, I saw him shut the car door like he

owned the place. His demeanor reminded me of the actor Edgar G. Robinson in *Barbary Coast*. Ironically, a movie about the same district of San Francisco.

Leaning against the sedan with studied nonchalance, he glanced around, then withdrew something from his pocket. It appeared to be a small notepad. Pencil in hand, he scanned the business fronts and made frequent jottings.

Mazzetti went into the joint closest to him, *The Pink Kitty*. Up until a couple of years ago, this place was raided by Vice regularly. Of late, it was considered legit and hands off with no explanation as to why.

I edged towards the front door, using a phone booth as cover when Mazzetti came out, tucking an envelope into his inner pocket. He scribbled some sort of mark in his book, then moved on to the next establishment.

An hour or so of watching him saunter in and out of the various clubs along the street, I realized, I could not let this continue, struggling to equate the Mazzetti getting riled up at the mere suggestion he could be bribed, with this Mazzetti running a protection racket.

Incredulously I shook my head and peeled out of the shadows.

I met the venerable lieutenant and family man extraordinaire, as he exited the *Hippodrome*. Grabbing my partner by the arm, I dragged him into a bar two doors down.

Thankfully, the time of day meant the place was empty. Most normal people were at work.

The bartender looked up from his newspaper and gave us a hairy eye when we entered. Doubtless, presuming we were a couple of lushes the way we stumbled past the bar without ordering drinks.

Finding a booth in the corner, I shoved Mazzetti into the seat, joined him, and jammed my service pistol into his ribs.

"What the hell, Jake?" Mazzetti spat.

"Hand it over, Lou," I ordered abruptly.

The expression on Mazzetti's face was priceless... and I thought the one he gave Zheng to be praiseworthy.

"Hand over what?"

Tired of his performance, I reached into his topcoat pocket and produced his notebook. Without removing the gun, I thumbed through a couple of pages.

The entries were cryptic at least, Lou's personal code at best:

PK: 150
LD: 100

...and so on.

"Spill it, Lou, what are you up to? Bearing in mind, I already have a good idea."

For a moment, genuine fear flickered in Mazzetti's eyes. He knew there was no way to convince me these were not bribes.

"Jake, please, you gotta understand. You know how hard it is to make ends meet on a cop's salary, especially with a family and house pay—"

"Can it, Lou. Don't try to pin this on Georgie. You're shaking down brothels for protection payoffs in exchange for looking the other way and tipping them off on upcoming raids... admit it. Zheng knew you were all bluster in his office, well aware you were on the take. That's why he dared to try to bribe you earlier."

If I expected my partner to break down and confess, perhaps beg for mercy, I was out of luck. Mazzetti's attitude took a one-eighty.

Calmly and implacably, he replied, "What are you going to do about it, Jake? I recall you were also offered that bribe. As for this little side venture of mine, do you honestly think Internal Affairs will believe you were clueless?

"You're my partner, Jake. Have been for years. So, why don't you take that peashooter out of my ribs and order us a couple of beers. Who knows, pal, play ya cards right, *behave yourself,* and I might find myself in the mood to cut you in."

I was tempted to pistol-whip the cheesy grin off his face. "Go fuck yourself, Mazzetti," I snapped, shoving my weapon in its holster.

Ignoring my suggestion, Mazzetti called to the bartender, "Two drafts."

Given murder was a capital offense, I left Mazzetti to enjoy both beers alone.

Mazzetti's blasé attitude to what was basically theft, rankled. Okay, I admit, I'm not perfect by any stretch of the imagination, but *this…* this left a nasty taste in my mouth. Made worse because he had me over a barrel, and he knew it. *Bastard.*

The drive home was not long enough to clear my head, and I needed the quiet of my apartment. It was not to be. I parked the De Soto in front of my building, and headed inside, to be met by my landlady, Esmeralda Harper.

Will this day never end?

"Mister Butterfield," the old lady slurred on a waft of rum. "If you intend to keep *that woman* in your room as more than an occasional guest, I will have to charge you for double occupancy. If you had bothered to read your lease *before* you took it upon yourself to move her in, you would know an extra person uses extra water, and heat."

I looked at the battle-axe, thinking wryly, *trust me you old biddy, we produce enough heat of our own to cover the cost,* and made do with a nod and a dismissive wave as I climbed the stairs to my room.

Her voice followed me like a bad headache. "I'm not running a flophouse here. This is a respectable place. Are you listening to me, Butterfield?"

Opening the door to my humble abode, I was greeted by the aroma of Turkish cigarettes.

Curled up on the coach, the voluptuous figure of one Stella Fitzhugh.

I am not sure how she came to be a roommate. I think it occurred after a night of heavy drinking. When I woke up the next morning, there she was, her unfamiliar cocktail waitress uniform strewn across the floor from the door to the bed.

I *do* remember checking the third finger on my left hand just to make sure I had not stupidly…

…thank God, no… but, at least she was easy on the eye and a good cook.

I dropped my coat and fedora on the adjacent armchair, seeing her eyes widen like a cat whose territory had been invaded.

"Perfume? You dare walk into my house smelling of a cheap whore?" she hissed.

"Calm down, Stella. I met with an informant this morning…" I countered mildly.

"Where? Her bedroom?"

I shook my head at her accusation, and, in need of a drink, grabbed a beer from the ice box, "…and since when was this *your* house? Last I looked, I'm the one paying rent and buying food."

I thought about pointing out I was covering the cost of her expensive choice in smokes as well but let it slide.

Popping the cap, I took a swig before tipping the bottom

of the bottle toward the door. "Feel free to use it anytime you want."

Realizing she had overplayed her hand, Stella let out a whimper worthy of a wounded kitten. She unfolded herself, rose to her feet, and sashayed over to me, letting her robe fall open, *accidentally*, to reveal her supple… and naked… curves.

Looping one arm around my neck, while stealing my beer and draining a good quarter of it, she kissed me on the chin. "I don't mean to get jealous, Jake, but you bring it out in me and, if I ever meet that woman, I'll scratch her eyes out."

"I doubt that'll ever happen." I chuckled, pressing my lips to her forehead.

Any shrink with half a mind to analyze our relationship would commit us both for being a danger to each other, but somehow, for us, it worked.

"Tell you what, Butterfield, how about we spend the rest of the day in bed, where you can make amends for your indiscretion?"

Arguing was a waste of time.

CHAPTER FOUR

My Friday with Stella stretched into late Sunday night. The ceaseless rain combined with a weekend off meant the only time we got out of bed was to replenish our strength with a one of Stella's amazing bacon and egg fry-ups, as the Brit's would say, complemented by a side order of rapidly vanishing beer.

Ok, so she squandered our week's ration of bacon in a couple of meals, but hey… what's life without the odd risk and, anyway, I reckoned we had earned it.

Monday morning rolled around. About to head to Clara's diner for breakfast, I spotted a soggy scrap of paper stuffed under the windscreen wiper of my car. Trying to keep it intact, I unfurled the note carefully, immediately recognizing the feminine handwriting. Mae's.

Hey darling,

Wanted to give you a heads up. There was a huge drama with the New York guys.

One minute they were there, the next they split.

The boss was pretty pissy about it, so much for a party, wouldn't want to be them for all the tea in China.

Anyway, we'll meet you for breakfast Monday and fill you in on the rest.

Your treat of course.

Kisses, M

"When is it not my treat?" I chuckled, tucking the note in my pocket.

I parked in front of Clara's and, checking my watch, smiled to see I was punctual, deciding to order two extra servings to avoid my own being pilfered by those two hussies.

That'll teach 'em.

Once inside, I was pleased to see my meal waiting at my customary spot. Making myself comfortable on the stool, I greeted, "Morning, Clara. May I order two more of the same?"

"Are you meeting those… those… *women* here again?" She spat the question disdainfully.

"'Fraid so. I need to talk to them."

"It took me all day to rid the place of their cheap perfume the last time. Besides, if you are in need of female companionship, I have a niece who's looking for a man."

"Tempting, hon, but this is strictly business."

Clara hmphed. "If you say so. Food'll be right out."

It was not long before two plates of food sat either side of me, reminiscent of Friday's food debacle.

I checked my watch. 7:10. *Where are they?*

By 7:20, I decided to call their place from the payphone. The phone rang out, no answer.

I tried again at 7:30. Still the same.

Returning to the counter, I found the hulking figure of Lou Mazzetti perched on the stool next to mine, helping himself to one of the untouched plates, not seeming to care it had long since gone cold.

"Why are you here?" I glared at him, resuming my seat.

"Weren't we planning to have breakfast this morning? I mean, you ordered all this food."

"After your threat on Friday, you're lucky I don't shoot you here and have Clara make you into chilli."

"That's harsh, partner," Mazzetti mumbled around the slice of bacon he had shoved in his mouth. Sipping from the tepid cup of coffee, he coaxed, "How about you forget what you saw the other day. It would be better for both of us."

He tugged a five from his wallet and dropped it on the counter, calling, "This should cover his bill, Clara… and keep the change," adding sarcastically, "Maybe you'll make sure his food is warm next time."

With that, he headed out to our assigned car, which I hadn't noticed was parked at the curb.

Ignoring Mazzetti's largesse — which equated to an entire day's profit for Clara — I paid for all three meals. "I'm sorry he's an ass, Clara. Do you mind if I leave my car out front?"

"Not a problem, Jake," she replied with a smile as she stuffed Mazzetti's five in her apron pocket. "It'll make the place look busy."

We shared a chuckle. Lack of business was one thing Clara never had to worry about.

"Thanks, I'll pick it up after my shift."

"Hey, for another five, I'll have the boys wash it for you."

"I'll pass," I said, draining the dregs of my coffee. "They'd probably wash the rust away with the mud, and she'll fall apart."

As I turned, I saw Mazzetti hurrying back to the diner. He pushed the door open, his voice booming off the walls, "Are you coming or what?"

Approaching the car, we heard dispatch crackling through the radio, "Control to Car 23, I repeat, Control to Car 23, report to the Wharf. Car with passengers being pulled from the bay."

By the time we arrived at the boat launch close to Fisherman's Wharf, the coroner had loaded the bodies into the back of the white transport wagon and was swinging the double doors shut.

"Mind if I take a look?" I asked him.

"Yeah, I do. They're not in the best shape. Been in this cesspool of a bay for a couple of days, and the local aquatic life has started taking bites. Come down to the morgue later. Gives you a chance to digest whatever you had for breakfast, because I don't want to clean it off my floor."

He walked to the driver's window, muttered something to the attendant, then nodded his farewell.

"Friendly sort, isn't he?" Mazzetti said, a toothpick clenched between his teeth.

I shrugged. "Bad enough we have to contend with the

crime scene, I couldn't imagine having to deal with the dead day in and out."

"Gotta be some sort of ghoul would be my guess. Bet he has a basement full of bodies."

I shot my partner a resigned look, before going to check on the waterlogged Ford coupe, whose doors hung open, all the windows rolled down, and Bay water still trickling out. "You're the last one to throw stones."

Officer Gulliver was overseeing the transportation of the car to the impound yard where it would be examined.

Standing next to him, I inquired, "What do we have here, Joey?"

"Hey, Sergeant," he greeted, his features sombre. "Looks like they were drunk and decided to park their car beside the Wharf… literally. Coroner thinks maybe early Saturday morning."

"You don't think it was foul play?" I asked as he closed his notebook.

"Nah, the coupe was chock full of empty bottles."

"Any idea who the car belongs to?"

Gulliver shook his head, "No, No registration. Need to check with Motor Vehicles… and we all know how quickly they get around to stuff."

We shared a laugh.

I tapped a cigarette from the pack in my coat pocket, and offered him one, which he refused, pointing out, "Ya know, those will kill ya."

Lighting up, I countered, "Better this way than seeing how long I can hold my breath in that water."

For a beat cop, Gulliver was pretty intuitive and not one for wild speculation. I expected him to take the detective's exam when it came up again. So, when he made an observation for my ears only, I listened intently.

"I think the car was stolen."

"Why do you think that?"

"If you'd seen the occupants, neither of them looked like they had a nickel between them."

"Friend's car maybe?"

"With no registration? Unlikely."

"Okay, Joey, thanks. I'll take that into consideration."

Joining Mazzetti at the coupe, the contents of which he was still fishing through, much to the annoyance of the tow truck driver who was waiting to hoist it up so he could be on his way. "What did your girlfriend whisper into your ear? Sweet nothings?"

"Nah, he said he left your wife satisfied for once... but I wasn't supposed to tell you. Oh, and you have a small penis."

"Want me to prove you wrong on that last part here and now?"

"Gulliver is a pretty honest guy so, I'll take his word." Before our conversation degenerated further, I asked, "Have you found anything worthwhile?"

The clattering of bottles came to an abrupt halt.

"Just as I thought," Mazzetti said triumphantly as he pulled a brick of something wrapped in brown kraft wax paper. "I'll bet you coffee it's drugs, most likely hashish."

It was only in the last year that the state of California and the federal government had deemed the substance dangerous and illegal.

"Sure, why not," I said, not bothering to hide my disinterest. I had been in Vice long enough to recognize it.

Mazzetti produced a pocketknife and slit it open. Unsurprisingly, it was as my partner suggested.

Curiously, although submerged for the last couple of days, the reddish-brown cannabis was dry, and I watched as, with a smug look, Mazzetti tucked the packet in his pocket.

Spotting my expression of concern, he reassured without breaking stride, "We'll log it into Evidence when we get back to the office."

"Make sure you do, Lou. Anything else of interest in there?"

"Nope, just enough empties to look like the pair was trying to consume a liquor store. My guess, if they hadn't drowned themselves, they would have died of alcohol poisoning."

"Let's see what the coroner finds before we make any assumptions. Until then, it's back to the office to file the report."

CHAPTER FIVE

After wasting the rest of the morning filling out reports, in triplicate, I reminded Mazzetti, "Don't forget to stop by the evidence room and log in the dope."

"Done." Mazzetti flashed what looked like an Evidence Document, then buried the sheet in the case file.

"When did you do that?" I arched a confused brow.

"When you took your morning constitutional." He added a useless tidbit of advice, "You really do need to cut back on Clara's greasy food. Can't be good for your gut."

I was about to defend my choice of sustenance when my phone rang.

"Butterfield, here." I answered, falling silent as I listened to the caller.

"Okay, thanks," I said, hanging up the receiver.

"What's up?" Mazzetti queried.

"Coroner wants us to stop by. Wasn't forthcoming on details."

"Well, let's not keep the poor man waiting," Mazzetti said with the smile I was finding more sickening each time he flashed it.

The ride to 650 Merchant Street, AKA the city morgue, was about as cheery as spending the night there. Neither of us spoke. By the time we reached the parking lot, I was finishing my fourth smoke of the morning. It helped curb my tongue.

Making our way to the basement, the aroma of formaldehyde grew stronger. I rifled through my pocket for the small container of menthol I kept there and rubbed the contents under my nose to kill the scent.

Against my better judgement, I offered it to Mazzetti, who accepted gladly.

"I never get used to the smell," he said.

I just nodded and walked through the morgue doors. Unwilling to interrupt the coroner, Hamilton Washington, who was tending to a body on a table at the far side of the room, we waited by the entrance.

After standing there awkwardly for a few minutes, I cleared my throat to catch his attention.

He glanced over. "Oh, hey boys." Removing his surgical gloves with a snap, Hamilton discarded them onto a metal tray next to him and smiled a greeting.

Signaling us to follow him, he crossed to a pair of examination tables, the body resting on each draped under a sheet.

"Like I warned you this morning, they aren't in the best shape." Washington pulled back the sheet on the first table to expose a female.

Blonde hair stringy and matted from immersion in the cold water, her right arm torn from the shoulder by what I assumed to be a shark bite. Most notable, blue eyes which twinkled playfully when she flirted, were now fixed lifelessly at the ceiling.

My heart sank as I registered her bluish-tinged lips and pallor.

It was Mae.

Unable to help myself, I lifted the sheet on the other table to expose June's upper body. Except escaping mutilation by rapacious sea-life, her condition was as distressing as her roommate.

Callously, Lou cracked, "Looks like they won't be joining you for breakfast tomorrow, or ever. Should save you a couple of bucks."

This unmitigated insensitivity proved the final straw, and the last threads of my patience snapped. I vented my fury in the form of a solid left hook. In my younger days, during the Great War, I had done some boxing, but that was twenty years ago.

I think I hurt my fist more than I hurt his granite-like jaw.

He rubbed his chin, that damned grin still on his face. "Easy, boy. Too late to do anything for them now."

He looked at the coroner — whose expression made his concern a brawl was about to break out in his orderly morgue abundantly clear — to ask, "Is there reason to believe this was anything other than a senseless drink driving accident?"

"The dark-haired one," the coroner pointed at June, "has a large contusion on the back of her head, but I think that happened when she hit the headliner of the car as it plunged it into the water."

"Wait," I broke in. "June—"

"That's her name?" Washington picked up a clipboard and jotted down the detail.

"Yeah, she is… or was… June Davies. Her roommate there was Mae Oliver."

Mazzetti interjected another unnecessary comment, "I

wouldn't bother trying to locate their next of kin, though. Names were probably aliases."

God, my hatred for this guy was growing with each breath he took.

I returned to the question I was trying to ask, "Hamilton, are you saying June was behind the wheel?"

"Yeah, like I say, I suspect she slammed her head against the roof when the car hit the water. Unusual but not unheard of."

He perused the notes on the clipboard and scratched his head, as though trying to determine whether his next words were pertinent.

"What is it?" I pressed.

"Given the number of empty bottles, if I had to sign off on this, I'd call it an open and shut case of death by drink driving. Both had alcohol in their bloodstream." He paused tapping his pen on the clipboard.

"That said, if the number of bottles equated to the amount of whisky they had drunk, I would expect to find a much higher alcohol to blood ratio, and am amazed… June did you say the driver was?" He looked at me, and I nodded. "…could see the car never mind drive it."

He shrugged, not in dismissal but in kind of morbid respect. "Just another example of the oddity of the body. I did find something strange. Both girls had freshwater in their lungs when I would expect salt."

"Meaning?" I needed clarification.

"Just a noteworthy anomaly. There are freshwater tributaries near where they entered the water, which may account for the lower salinity level." He had no need to add the 'but' — I heard it loud and clear, and tucked it away to be revisited later, if necessary.

Impatiently, Mazzetti pressed, "So, did these two hookers die accidentally or not?"

"Oh, yeah," Washington conceded. "I'll rule it as misadventure."

"Thanks, Hamilton." Mazzetti slapped the coroner on the shoulder. "If there is nothing else, Jake, can we get the hell out of here?"

Before I could tell him to hold his horses, Mazzetti was on his way out of the morgue, leaving Washington and me staring at each other. Mazzetti's haste was unusual even for him, and something nudged at the back of my brain, gone before I could pin it down. Doubtless it would come back to me if it was important.

I asked Washington a question to which I already knew the answer, "What will the city do with the bodies?"

Returning to the body he was attending to when we first arrived, the coroner replied, "Cremation and their ashes scattered on the bay." He paused for a second, then said with gallows humor, "I guess we could have just left them there in the first place, huh?"

Ignoring this, I placed a business card on the stand next to him. "Before you do, let me know. I want to make arrangements for a decent burial in the cemetery in Colma."

"Sure, sure," Washington agreed absently, his focus on the task in front of him.

"And…this is just between you and me."

Washington glanced at me, nodded, and went back to work.

Climbing back into our car, I did not wait for Mazzetti to open his damned mouth again, and demanded, "Why are you in so much of a hurry to write Mae and June off?"

"Because the higher-ups aren't gonna give a damn about dead hookers."

"What about the car they were in? You know the girls as much as I do, and you know June would never be caught…" the following word tugged at me, "*dead* driving anything other than her hunk of junk *Maxwell*."

"They were drunk… so who knows what they were thinking. Anyway, Washington is satisfied with his findings, and so am I. Case closed. You need to let it go. I'm hungry and, after that sucker punch, you're buying."

CHAPTER SIX

The coupe fished out of the bay was not claimed by its owner until Friday.

The Ford was rented from a company at the Los Angeles Municipal Airport the previous week, to be returned to the San Francisco Airport on Monday.

When the customer failed to return the rental by Wednesday, it was listed as stolen with the California Highway Patrol. Subsequently, our request for a match on the plates came up as a hit.

Since the city had closed the investigation relating to the deaths of Mae and June, the brass saw no reason not to return the wrecked car to its rightful owner who, in turn, handed it over to their insurance company along with a claim for reimbursement.

Once in possession of the insurance company, the vehicle's fate was out of our hands and was probably scrapped or sold to some dodgy used car dealership in Tijuana, Mexico. That this was concluded in a neat and orderly fashion over the weekend was no comfort, given its removal deprived us of any evidence the car might contain.

Monday morning, I was at my desk at a ridiculously early hour. I had forgone my usual stop at Clara's. Knowing I would be eating by myself was too much to take.

I distracted myself by rereading the coroner's report and the auto theft report. June must have had her foot pressed down hard on the gas pedal when she hit the water to produce the massive head wound Hamilton had detailed.

As for the rental, it was signed out by an Otto Driver… *cute, huh?*… from Queens, New York. Of course, neither the name nor listed address were genuine.

I placed a call to the rental agency in LA hoping to get a description of the mysterious Mr. Driver, to be informed he was a large, brooding man.

While not much to go on, it did not come as much of a surprise that the description sounded similar to the one Zheng provided. The longer I studied the file, the more clues I registered, leading me to conclude that the hit man who gunned down the two suits in Chinatown had murdered Mae and June.

Tossing the papers on the desk, I decided to check out the girls' apartment. Given the San Francisco Police Department had accepted the coroner's findings of accidental death there was no authorization, but what my superiors did not know would not hurt them… and, by extension, me.

Also, my pain in the ass partner was conspicuous by his absence, so I was left to my own devices. Not that I was complaining. I was not in the mood to justify my actions to him, or anyone.

At the end of my shift, I headed to the Tenderloin District, and Mae and June's place. The sun had set over the Pacific shrouding the city in twilight and, as I drove into the neighborhood, the minimal illumination in these narrower streets, along with the shadows shed by tall buildings, added to the gloom.

One of the few streetlights stood in front of the girls' apartment building, and under it sat June's black car, waiting patiently for its owner to return.

Recalling her telling me she had jammed the key in the ignition, I slid inside and spotting the key still stuck, turned it. The Maxwell sputtered and grumbled but fired up easily enough.

Okay, so why were they cruising town in that coupe? As with the coroner's findings, this made no sense, and I slotted it into the same folder at the back of my head. Two and two were not making four.

Killing the engine, I entered the building and climbed the rickety stairs to their fourth-floor apartment.

Their door stood ajar. I froze on the threshold, listening intently, but any movement within was masked by the background noise echoing around the internal walls.

My .38 in hand, I pushed the door, pistol pointing into the darkened interior. Knowing better than to step into an unknown scene... unlike the foolhardy detectives in the movies... I stretched my arm around the doorframe to toggle the switch. The bare bulb, hanging by its cord from the ceiling, lit the apartment.

The girls were not interior decorators by any stretch of the imagination. Two large red velvet sofas, circa last century, a dinette set, and a queen-size bed. Surprisingly, the place had a separate bathroom.

Which sounded as though it was occupied.

Creeping to the door, I pressed myself against the wall

and jiggled the doorknob. Two bullets pierced the wood. Giving the shooter no chance to follow with a third, I put my big foot to the door, smashing it into the small room, and slamming it into a large man. The impact knocked him sideways into the clawfoot bath.

With a thud, he struck his head against the enamel coated, cast iron rim, a frying pan, he was holding for some unknown reason, clattered on the tiles.

His finger shaking, he raised his pistol in an attempt to fire again and, employing a nimble move, of which Errol Flynn would be envious, I scooped up the pan and swatted the gun out of his hand.

It tumbled to the floor, and I drove the barrel of my weapon into his left temple.

"SFPD, aka your worst nightmare," I informed him, my voice dripping with venom. "Unless you want the wax cleaned out of your ears permanently, I suggest you tell me what the hell you're doing here."

"Go fuck yourself, copper," the intruder spat, his New York accent unmistakable.

Blood from the laceration on the right side of his head dripped into the tub.

I cocked the hammer on my .38, the metallic click filling the cramped quarters. "Care to try that again?" My tone telling him I was in no mood for games. "Who are you and what are you doing here?"

The who, I guessed was the mysterious Otto Driver. The what? That was up for discussion.

"Look, hotshot, either pull the trigger, or get that hogleg out of my ear. You ain't no killer. 'Cuz if you were, I'd be dead already, knowing what I did to your *girlfriends*. Even if you're a clean cop... *not* the word on the street... I can't imagine you being this broke up about a coupla whores."

"Don't push it," I warned, gritting my teeth, my finger tightening around the trigger.

"Ya have no idea how easy it was to get in their apartment. Shit, after flashing a bit of cash at them, they begged me to join 'em." The smarmy smile on his face tested my rapidly evaporating self-restraint.

"Shame I had to brain the brunette in the head with the frypan, but I couldn't drown 'em both in the tub at the same time. That damn frypan. My only mistake. If I hadn't forgotten it, I would'na had to traipse back to this fleabag joint."

I flipped it over to see specks of blood and strands of black hair clinging to the scorched and battered base.

I withdrew the barrel from his temple but did not lower the gun.

Rage burned, threatening to consume me, causing my hand to shake. I bit out, "You didn't have to kill either of them."

"Wasn't my call," he shrugged, relaxed marginally, and used a handkerchief he twitched from the breast pocket of his suit coat to staunch the blood oozing from his head.

"Then, who?"

"People who want this war... and not just the local gang war. The world is about to explode, and whoever controls the necessary resources, and the means to sell to both sides, will come out of this richer than you can imagine. Much as I would like to help," his sardonic sneer implying the opposite, "their identities are above my pay grade, and they have their limits."

Light dawned. Mae and June were collateral damage. Eliminated to prevent them from revealing what they had seen or heard. Were there others? I do not believe in coincidences. My hunch was correct... the two guys murdered in

Chinatown *had* to be connected. Were more bodies going to pop up at random over the next few days?

Nonchalantly, Driver glanced at his .45 lying just out of reach on the tiles. I caught the motion and, smiling grimly, pocketed my pistol, hit him across the cheek with the pan, then dropped it to scoop up his automatic.

"You're so right, man, and I've reached my limit."

His eyes widened when the hammer clicked in his ear, before falling with a deafening *BANG*. The slug burrowed through his head to burst out of the other side, along with a decent portion of his skull.

The metal fragment lodged into the wall… or into whatever was in the adjacent apartment. Blood and brain matter splattered the wall and dribbled down into the tub.

Without haste, I holstered my .38 and grabbed a washcloth hanging on the rail to wipe the .45 clean.

No sense giving the forensic boys any evidence linking this to me.

Cleaning my prints off the frying pan handle, I tucked it into Driver's hand and closed his fingers around it tightly, before replacing it with his gun.

The scene looked staged, but I didn't care. At least Mae and June got the justice no one else in San Francisco felt they deserved.

I removed my prints from anything I may have touched tonight, aware I had been in the apartment too frequently to erase them all.

In case anyone had decided to check on the disturbance, I paused on the threshold of the apartment, but this was the Tenderloin District. Gunshots here were as common as the nightly weather report.

Descending to the street, I got into my car, mulling over Driver's words. I had become the very thing I fought against, the lowest of the low — a corrupt cop and a murderer. Did I regret my actions? That remained to be seen.

I shifted the automobile into gear and drove off.

CHAPTER SEVEN

It was about half past ten when I parked the DeSoto in front of my building. Stella met me at the door of my apartment. It did not take a genius to deduce what I had been up to; my coat and shirt were covered in blood.

You do not shoot somebody at point-blank range and avoid blow-back.

I saw questions flicker in her eyes, but instead of voicing them, she led me to the shower.

Turning on the water, she let it run until the bathroom filled with steam, then instructed, "Wash yourself thoroughly, and I mean scrub."

I stripped out of my suit and did as I was told.

The water rinsed away all traces of blood and, hopefully, any gunshot residue from my hand, down the drain. After a good fifteen minutes, and feeling the temperature of the water drop, I turned off the shower, grabbed a towel, and dried myself.

Stella had collected my suit and replaced it with a pair of pyjamas. Dressed, I opened the bathroom door, catching a whiff of lighter fluid and smoke.

The window leading to the fire escape stood open, I poked my head out to see Stella had started a fire in the trash can and was burning my suit.

So much for that $12.95.

She shot me a quick glance, and instructed me to, "Get the towel and washcloth. Everything goes."

I retrieved the last of the evidence, which she dropped onto the flames. Hopefully, anyone along the street who spotted the can would assume we were toasting marsh-mallows.

Silently, Stella passed me to climb back into the apartment. "I'm heading for bed. Make sure the fire goes out properly before you join me."

Without a second thought, my unofficial live-in girlfriend had become an accessory after the fact to murder.

Would Stella save her hide at my expense?

Entering the Homicide Squad room the next morning, I was still wondering whether Stella would vouch for me if push came to shove. An answer only time would reveal.

I draped my coat over my chair and sat down to flip through the stack of papers on my desk. I was looking for a murder report from the Tenderloin District. Specifically, one relating to an unidentified man found in a recently unoccupied apartment. To my amazement there was nothing.

Those walls were thin, and the gunshot was loud; somebody must have heard it.

I thought about asking Mazzetti, but a glance across my desk found my *trusted* partner acting hinky and avoiding eye contact.

Arching a brow, and about to open my mouth, I heard Captain O'Connor call my name.

"Butterfield. In here now."

As I rose to head into the office, in which all the blinds were closed, I heard Mazzetti mutter, "Jake, it wasn't me. I swear."

"You swear what, Lou?" The hairs on my nape prickled. That same niggle, the one which began in the bar, and magnified by his behaviour at the morgue, resurfaced. *What had he done?*

"Butterfield. Now," O'Connor barked before Mazzetti could reply and I spied a strange expression of relief sweep over his face.

I walked into the captain's domain, to see him standing at the window, staring out at the street, his back to me.

"Close the door behind you." An order he did not need to issue twice.

A weasel of a man in a rumpled, ill-fitting, shit-brown suit, leaned against the wall in the corner. Lieutenant Rudolph Wells flashed a smile as greasy as his slicked thinning salt and pepper hair.

The man from Internal Affairs looked like one of those wanna-be gangsters in the movies, and everyone gave him a wide berth, as though he carried the plague. It was rumored, if he showed up in an office, someone was getting fired, or worse, going to jail.

I knew, as far as he was concerned, he preferred the latter for me. He had been bound and determined to consign me to a 9ft x 5ft cell in Alcatraz since the day I collared his city council brother-in-law in a brothel bust.

He might, at the very least, be satisfied with the much smaller, but no less spurious, 8 x 10 inch in cheap wood, if it meant ridding the SFPD of me.

At the soft click of the door shutting, O'Connor broke his silence.

"You and Mazzetti are off the gang war investigation. J. Edgar Hoover is assigning it to his boys."

Why, Captain?" I asked, failing to sound as astonished as his statement warranted, recalling Mazzetti's remark about informing the Feds in order to keep our hands clean.

"Because my superiors, informed by the governor, who was ordered by J. Edgar, say so. If you have any complaints, I suggest you take it up with President Roosevelt."

I glanced over my shoulder at Wells. "Can I ask why he is here, Captain?"

"Sergeant Butterfield," Wells interposed smoothly... too smoothly. "I am glad you asked. There are a couple of indiscretions I need help to understand."

"Indiscretions?" I repeated.

With an annoyingly purposeful stride, Wells crossed the room to O'Connor's desk and picked up a folder which I could see was filled with an assortment of papers, and photographs.

"Let's start with an easy one, Sergeant." He pulled out two pictures. One of Mae and the other of June. Morgue photos, originals. "Can you identify these two women?"

"You damn well know who they are, Wells."

"Then can you tell me how *exactly* you knew them?"

"They were my informants. The entire office was aware of that." I turned my attention to the captain, "Sir, I don't see how this has anything to do—"

O'Connor remained impassive, as Wells interrupted caustically, "On the topic of them acting as your informants, I put it to you that they were unwilling participants, and only complied because you offered them protection from arrest in exchange for dirt?"

"No way. Where did you hear that rubbish?" I contested hotly.

"Is it not also true you were shaking down businesses along the Barbary Coast?" Referring to 'Frisco's red-light district, *not* certain coastal regions of North Africa.

More pictures tumbled from the folder, scattering across the captain's desk. Some were taken through the window at Clara's Diner when the girls had breakfast with me. Others from the day I had discovered Mazzetti's dirty little secret. More telling… he was not in any of them.

Who the hell had taken them? Mazzetti? Maybe the ones at the diner, but the day I followed him, it was physically impossible for him to be in two places at once. The nebulous unease increased, and warning bells clanged in my head.

Something was badly wrong here. I was the one being called to the carpet and not my partner. Had I been set up from the start, were others in cahoots with Mazzetti? So much for an 8x10 — the frame was shrinking by the second.

A somber picture of two freshly dug graves in the Cypress Lawn Memorial Park in Colma was thrust into my hand.

"Can you tell me who paid to bury two whores in such a nice place? According to their records, it was a Mr. John Smith. If I was a gambling man, Butterfield, my guess is that you were their benefactor. No doubt owing to a guilty conscience for causing their death."

"Hey, hold it right there… it isn't like that." I tried to defend myself.

"So, you have no remorse for their deaths? Interesting." Wells folded his arms.

"That's a leap," I retorted, striving to control my fraying temper, and the burning desire too slap the smarmy grin of his aggravating face, "and my feelings aside, the powers that be ruled their deaths were a result of drink driving."

"Your actions have led us to review those findings. Furthermore, we can produce a number of sex workers from the area prepared to testify to your involvement in extortion and bribery. All of which pales into insignificance when compared with the main reason I was compelled to interrupt my busy day, not to mention Captain O'Connor's."

He removed the last piece of paper from the folder, and paused, presumably for dramatic effect, which was totally wasted on his audience.

"Did you find a kilo of Hashish in the car pulled from the San Francisco Bay?"

"To correct you, Lieutenant, my partner Louis Mazzetti did," I pointed out.

"Which you noted in the report, yes?" Wells countered.

"Of course."

That's when I fell into his trap.

"So, can you tell me why only half a kilo was logged?"

"Don't ask me," I shot back. "Ask my goddamned partner. Mazzetti took responsibility for that."

Wells flapped the sheet in front of my face. "Then explain your signature on the log and not his?"

I snatched the sheet and studied it. There at the bottom of the paper was the signature of yours truly. Sloppily written admittedly, but close enough to make it hard to refute with anything more than a stunned, "I didn't sign it in. Louis Mazzetti did. Go ask him yourself."

O'Connor spoke at long last, sounding like my father being forced to admonish me for some imagined atrocity, "We did, Jacob. He said you insisted on logging it as soon as you returned, and the guys in Evidence backed him up."

I felt the color drain from my face, and ice slither down my spine — an impressive feat given my white-hot outrage. I recalled Mazzetti's smug face when he pocketed the brick and, later, the waved paperwork along with his blithe assurance that he had handed it in. It was my own stupid fault for trusting him. I swallowed a coarse expletive as, mentally, I slapped my forehead for not accompanying him to Evidence.

The snake.

Disbelief mingled with my fury. Shit, it was true. For the right price, the entire SFPD could be bought.

"Captain, please…" Stupefied, my brain refused to cooperate with my mouth. How the hell had it come to this?

"I am sorry, Sergeant Butterfield," O'Connor said, dropping the final shoe. "Pending further investigation, you are officially suspended without pay. Weapon and badge, please."

And that was that. Sacked! They could dance around the appellation but, to all intents and purposes, I was without gainful employment. Even if the charges came to nothing, who would trust me again? My integrity, my credibility were ruined. I wanted to pound Mazzetti to a pulp then punch him into next month.

Turning to leave the office, Wells cautioned snidely, "Do not think about leaving town until you hear from us."

I slammed the door behind me with as much force as I could muster, drawing the attention of every cop in the bullpen. Their accusatory whispers followed me to my desk, where a uniformed officer handed me my jacket asking, I had to assume, rhetorically, "Nothing else you need from here?" Then escorted me out.

As we passed Mazzetti, I warned in a fierce undertone, "This is not over."

CHAPTER EIGHT

On the verge of alcohol poisoning, I made it back to my apartment sometime before sunrise. I had crawled through every cheap dive and gin joint in the seedier parts of the city to drink my sorrows away.

Stumbling through my door, I was greeted by the sounds of the city below. Looking for its source, I realised the window to the fire escape was open. A glance at the couch, where my queen usually perched, suggested she had taken up residence on the makeshift balcony instead.

The scent of her Turkish cigarette wafted through the apartment. For her to be smoking this late… or early… did not bode well.

Warily, I poked my head through the window to see her sitting on one of the steps up from our landing, a pensive expression on her beautiful face.

"Penny for your thoughts?" I slurred, the alcohol reassuring me I was being charming.

"Out killing more people tonight, Jacob?" she replied in a tone devoid of emotion.

"Just my liver, doll."

"Why didn't you just come home after you got canned?" Stella asked, taking the last drag of her cigarette, then crushing it out among the dozen or so other stubs in her ashtray.

"H-how did you know," I stammered, startled.

"Mazzetti called…"

Good ol' Lou Mazzetti, my caring *friend.*

"…looking for you. He told me what happened. Why did I have to hear it from *him* instead of you?"

I tried to circumvent the question. "Did he want anything else?"

"No, that was pretty much all," she said to the cool predawn, then faced me. "Answer the question, Jake."

"Because I'm a coward, I guess."

"I contemplated leaving you this evening." She rose to her feet and stretched. "Still am. Mind, helping you cover up a murder makes that a little harder."

"I'd never jeopardize your freedom, Stella—"

She did not appear to be listening anymore. "Get some sleep, Jake. We'll talk more later." Gliding passed me, she brushed my cheek with her hand. Her touch was almost ghostly, like an omen.

I was hard pushed to suppress a shudder

She left me on the fire escape, and something about her demeanor made me think she was about to abandon me too.

I forced my eyes open, trying to focus on the ceiling. I had no idea how long I was unconscious, but my aching, spinning head told me it was not nearly long enough.

Rolling over, I stretched out my hand, expecting to stroke Stella's soft skin, to be met by cold, empty sheets. An unexpected surge of sadness swamped me, suspecting my premonition was right, that she had wised up and fled during the night.

No more than I deserved.

I rose from the bed on unsteady feet. I glanced at the nightstand expecting to see the proverbial *Dear John* letter but there was nothing there.

Didn't I deserve even that consideration? I thought, wallowing in self-pity.

Shuffling through the bedroom door, the scent of desperately needed liquid strength greeted me, along with the surprising sight of Stella Fitzhugh who to my scarcely concealed astonishment, had swapped her silk kimono for something far more impressive. Something, I did not think possible.

The woman seated at the table was wearing what I guessed to be, in my extremely limited knowledge of female attire, a floral power dress. Her hair was swept up and secured under a pillbox hat. At first, I thought she was either on her way to a job interview or a date with a sugar daddy.

I was wrong on both counts.

Putting down the paper she was reading, she cut me a look which informed me she meant business, then lit the last cigarette in her pack, and offered it to me. "Your need is greater than mine."

Stella knew I hated the taste of those damn smokes but, given she had decided to stay, if only for the moment, I accepted.

Pouring myself a cup of coffee, I took a quick drag on the cigarette, then rinsed the taste from my mouth with a slurp.

Stella sat back in her chair to study me. "How long are you *suspended*?" The emphasis on her last word told me she believed the SFPD had dismissed me rather than the official line of being on leave without pay.

"Until they're done with whatever they are investigating and decide to call me back." Unwisely, I tried to ease the mood with an ill-timed joke. "Ya know don't call us. We'll call you."

Stella was not amused.

"Is there anything they can pin on you, Jake? Like a murder?"

"No. In fact, it looks like nobody reported anything. I think we are safe in that regard."

"What do they think they have?"

"Corruption and bribery. I'm accused of accepting money to look the other way by the pimps along the Coast."

"Christ, Butterfield, I told you to stay away from those whores," Stella chastised, following it up with, "Did you?"

"Did I what?" My head was in no shape for twenty questions.

"Don't play the idiot with me. You're skating on thin ice. Did you take any money?"

"You know me better than that, Stell. If I had, wouldn't I have a nicer joint?"

"Hard to tell. You're a cheapskate." It was her turn to dole out the bad humor and, despite the throbbing in my skull, I chuckled, because it was true.

"Oh, there was one more thing." I sobered.

"I am afraid to ask," Stella swiped her smoldering cigarette from my fingers.

"Half a kilo of dope is missing from the Evidence Locker."

"Sweet Jesus, Jacob, what have you been doing?"

"Not dealing drugs. Mazzetti was the one who checked it in, but the jerk signed my name on the log."

"You have been royally screwed, my love."

The term of affection took me aback. It was the first time she had used that endearment, but I opted not to read anything into it. I could not take another hit.

"We both know that call is never coming, even though they don't have enough evidence to convict. That said, we need to generate some form of income. I have grown accustomed to a certain lifestyle, you know."

"You mean me paying for everything."

"Tomato. Tomahto," Stella countered airily in an eerie echo of June's reference to last year's Fred Astaire movie. "Anyway, I've been looking through the papers for office space—"

"*Office* space?" I repeated dazedly. "Are you going into business?"

Showing me the *Want* ads, she shook her head, stubbing out the smoke. "Not hardly. You are."

"Doing?" It was like pulling teeth.

"You're a cop, yes? At least, you were."

"Thanks for reminding me that's in the past tense."

"Stop sulking," Stella ordered. "We're gonna do the next best thing and make you San Francisco's best PI. First, we need an office you can afford, then, on Monday, we'll go to Sacramento to get your license. If you're a good boy, I might let you buy me dinner while we are there…and a night in a hotel."

"My treat, eh?" I quirked an amused bow and shook my head.

"Only fair. I came up with the plan."

"You do recall I am not supposed to leave town without permission." I felt it important to remind her of Wells' caveat.

"What Wells doesn't know…" she started airily.

"…won't hurt him," I finished and grinned suddenly lighter of heart.

CHAPTER NINE

We spent the better part of Saturday afternoon trudging in and out of various office buildings, looking for a suitable place to set up shop. By the second, I was over it, a wooden fruit crate under the Golden Gate Bridge would suffice.

My intrepid, self-appointed, office manager would not hear of such a thing.

"If I am going to work in your office, it must be to my liking," she admonished. "I shall also require a proper desk."

"Pray tell, Miss Rockefeller, how do you propose we pay for everything?"

A wicked smile, unlike one I had ever seen on that beautiful face, curved her lips. "Never you mind, Butterfield, I have that taken care of."

I eyed her suspiciously. "You're not going to make me stand on the street corner, are you?"

Stella laughed. "You should know by now, I don't share my toys."

Over a late lunch, we reviewed the rest of the list. Most of the decent offices were located proximate to a higher class of prospective clientele but the rent was prohibitive. A cloud descended over the table.

"Looks like that fruit crate is becoming a viable option," I lamented, not wholly in jest.

Pulling a cigarette from her case, Stella waited for me to light it, while she studied one of the ads in the paper.

In my best gentlemanly fashion, I flipped open my *Ronson* lighter and held the flame under the tip of her smoke. "Shall I light your nose as well?" Vying with the newspaper for her attention.

"Sure," she said absently, still reading.

"Earth to Stella." I refrained from tapping her on the forehead but only just. "Mind telling me what's made you deaf to the threat of a flambéed beak?"

"Hmm?" she replied, without lifting her head. "Are you opposed to an office on Sanchez?"

"The Mission District? Hell, I'd be safer under the Bridge. Would probably smell better too."

"Come on, Jacob. You're a big boy who can take care of himself. Let's check it out. I promise it will be the last one today."

The description did sound enticing. Spacious office, incredible view of the old city — if you ignored the vagrants roaming the streets — and the best part, utilities included.

Before I could object, Stella was heading for the door. She paused by the entrance and glanced over her shoulder shooting me her, *well, are you coming?* look. Dropping a couple of dollars on the table, I followed behind like a good puppy.

While I might not have enunciated my reservations before we left the cafe, I could not curb my tongue on the drive to 22nd and Sanchez.

The building was old and tired to the point, I reread the ad, certain we were in the wrong place. Once upon a time, this structure might have represented the burgeoning wealth of the city's society; the numerous offices, providing a variety of essential services to the local community. No longer bustling with people, its current aspect was one of gloomy neglect.

We climbed the staircase, noting how many former offices were being used as storage. One was occupied by an insurance company I had never heard of. The door stood ajar revealing a receptionist sitting behind a desk reading a magazine.

She glanced up as we passed but did not speak.

The third floor housed a talent agency, and that was being kind, auditioning a singer who could not find the right note had it been pinned to his lapel, along with a couple of other offices whose function was not obvious from the nameplates, and I could not be bothered to waste time speculating.

On the top floor, we came to a door which opened onto a large space. The expansiveness did not seem to fit the motif of the building's other shoebox offices which surrounded it.

Almost filling the opposite wall, a stained-glass window, split into three sections — a graceful arch above two rectangles set side by side.

The design resembled a Tiffany lamp, the gem-like colors sending rainbows spilling over the floor, creating a welcoming ambience.

The place was vacant, except for a rotund gentleman...

and I use that term loosely… wearing a green-checked, linen suit, and chasing a mouse across the floor. By the sweat stains spreading on his jacket, and his beet-red face, he had been on the losing end of this particular battle for some time.

Stella cleared her throat, catching the man's attention. The mouse seized the opportunity to scurry into the nearest hole.

The balding man who appeared to be in his fifties, cursed the creature as it escaped his clutches.

Pulling a handkerchief from his pocket, he mopped the sweat from his brow, and *then* his hand, which he extended to Stella, as he introduced himself, "Good afternoon, I am Ramone Perez."

Fighting not to curl her lip in distaste, my newly minted office manager looked at him, then at his still damp open palm. Clamping her arm against her side, she simply nodded an acknowledgment. "I'm sure."

Without skipping a beat, she broke into the negotiation song and dance like a desert trader. "Is this the space listed in the paper?"

Perez glanced around, a broad, cheesy smile lighting his face. "Aye, it was occupied previously by a stock investor. He stood by that window every day," adding under his breath, "until Black Tuesday."

I was not sure whether he realized his costly mistake before he caught himself. "That is, until he was relocated by his company."

His slip of the tongue gave us two vital facts. Firstly, the previous tenant probably took a swan-dive out the fourth-story window when the market crashed in '29.

Secondly, and more importantly, the office had been empty for the last nine years.

I guess suicide reduces the attraction.

Stella had the same idea, and bargained, "We'll take the

office at a twenty percent discount. Dare balk at it, and it will go to twenty-five."

Perez fell silent.

I had to assume that, no matter how he parsed the numbers, eighty percent of something was better than one hundred percent of nothing.

"Fine," he huffed. "But you're signing a two-year lease."

He was not capitulating without a fight.

"Agreed," Stella said. "As long as you hire an exterminator to get rid of the mice."

"B-but do you have any idea—"

"By Tuesday," Stella's adamant reply ended the discussion.

The man nodded, wiped his hand on the last dry spot on his jacket, and extended it once more. This time Stella shook it.

"Do you have any furniture? You know desks, filing cabinets, and such like."

"Not yet." The smile Stella bestowed on him was calculated to slay him. "I don't suppose you know where we can find some?"

Mission accomplished! Duly dazzled, Perez, the sluggish cogs in his brain beginning to whirr with the hope he might yet salvage something from the deal, hurried us down to one of the storage rooms which was stuffed full of discarded office equipment.

In less than an hour, Stella had commandeered enough furniture to furnish a couple of rooms, along with a bed. *Why a bed?* I was not game to ask.

"Make sure you have this in our place by Wednesday, after the mice are gone," she reminded him.

"When can I expect payment?" Perez inquired.

"When you finish your chores," Stella retorted over her shoulder, took my arm, and had me escort her from the building.

The rest of the weekend was reasonably uneventful. I prepared the necessary paperwork to take to Sacramento to get my PI license, while Stella packed what seemed to me to be an inordinate number of clothes for so brief a visit, *not* that I was dim-witted enough to pass comment.

On Sunday afternoon, she went out muttering vaguely about picking up some medicinal items from the market.

I had no idea this was possible. Most places were prohibited from operating on Sundays under the antiquated Blue Laws.

She returned an hour or so later, looking supremely satisfied with herself — if a little flushed.

Taking a seat at the table, she opened her purse and extracted a wad of bills.

I scrutinized the bundle, then eyed her warily. "Care to explain?"

The smile she sent me was an unsettling blend of demure and cunning. "Yesterday, you asked how we were going to pay for everything. I knew you'd come up with the same idea, I just beat you to it."

"Beat me to what, my dear?" A headache niggled.

"Fleecing the golden goose. After what you told me about the extracurricular activities of a certain Lieutenant Louis Mazzetti, I figured he would be in no position to turn down a rare yet..." she paused and canted her head, "...irresistible investment opportunity."

"You mean you're blackmailing him."

"Semantics, Jake, semantics."

"Be careful, Stella. He can be dangerous if you back him into a corner."

"Don't worry, hon. I believe his desire to be a free family

man far exceeds his aspirations to be a crooked cop, and land himself in jail."

I was about to reiterate my caution, but she vanished into the bedroom to change into a pair of sailor-style slacks in navy blue, teamed with a blue and white figure-hugging top…a la Joan Crawford. The ensemble was highlighted by a large floppy white hat and sunglasses.

For some reason, I forgot what we were discussing.

Reading me like a book, she lowered the sunglasses proactively. "I don't know what you have in mind, Mr. Butterfield, but that coupe of yours won't pack itself."

CHAPTER TEN

The optional radio I had let the salesman talk me into when I first purchased the *Six* proved to be a welcome inclusion on the two-hour drive from San Francisco to Sacramento.

Between the news and occasional music programs, it was just enough to drown Stella's chatter regarding what we required for the office, as well as the need to advertise.

To me, advertising was being listed in the yellow pages.

The DeSoto wound its way along Route 50 towards the capital. Farmland, orchards, and vineyards dotted the landscape. I was forced to stop at various points so my traveling companion could purchase bushels of oranges, peaches, and almonds.

Not satisfied with fruit and nuts, she also splashed out on a bottle of wine or three from the small roadside vineyards to celebrate our new partnership.

Eventually, loaded down like a farmer going to market, we reached the Sacramento Valley, and the capital of California. The capitol building, our destination for tomorrow, sat proudly in the middle of the city.

Needing a bed for the duration, we drew up at an innocuous travel court along the highway whose only claim to fame was a small pool, something Stella insisted on. The brightly lit vacancies sign boded well.

Like a child at the circus, Stella was through the gate, kicking off her sandals, and dipping her toes into the water before I had killed the engine.

This, of course, left me to complete the formalities of asking about a room, checking in, and unloading our luggage.

I was hauling the last of her suitcases into the small cabin when she appeared at the door, "Jacob, hurry and change into your swimming trunks…"

She deposited her hat on the bed, and began shedding her clothes as she spoke, the door wide open, and something I hastened to take care of to avoid her being arrested for indecent exposure.

Undeterred, she stood before me naked, smiling mischievously, "...the water is simply heavenly."

Needless to say, it was a little while before we made it to the pool.

I am a red-bloodied male, after all.

Sometime later, looking more or less presentable, we grabbed two glasses from the bureau, one of the bottles of wine, and wandered outside.

We lounged by the pool, enjoying the peace of the early evening until a husband and wife, shepherding five screaming banshees, ruined the tranquility.

Stella clicked her tongue in disdain. "That is why I shall never have any of those."

Having a family was not something I had considered. Being a cop did not lend itself to a happy marriage, although, to be fair, some made it work. Neither had I met anyone with whom I wanted to spend the rest of my life, not even Stella, and becoming a PI was not likely to alter the status quo. In fact, it would probably be even more disruptive.

There was no chance to discuss it further because Stella... perhaps deliberately... collected her belongings and stalked off, tossing over her shoulder, "I'm hungry. Feed me."

Monday morning found us standing in front of a door emblazoned in gold leaf, announcing we had reached the California Department of Consumer Affairs. From the other side, the deafening clatter of multiple typewriters keys being struck by countless fingers echoed into the hallway.

Except for an elderly woman who manned the Information Desk, no one looked up from their work when we opened the door.

"May I help you?" she asked, her voice a raspy drawl from age and too many cigarettes.

"Yes, ma'am," I replied in my most professional police sergeant tone. "My name is Jacob Butterfield, and I wish to apply for my Private Investigator's License."

That won me a suspicious once over.

"Fill out this paperwork and return to my window when you are finished," she commanded, piling enough sheets of paper to rival Tolstoy's *War and Peace*. "You do know how to read and write, yes?"

"Yeah," I huffed. "I think I can manage. Besides, that's why she's here." I jerked my head at Stella who gave a sweet smile.

"I'm afraid she is *not* allowed to assist you, sir," she

retorted. "The state needs to know you have a modicum of education."

"Sure, sure," I acknowledged, lifting the stack. "If I get stuck, I'll draw a picture."

The morning slipped by as I answered a litany of inane questions such as… *Have you ever been convicted of a felony? If so, how many and why?*

Why what? Why did I commit the crime, or why was I caught?

When I muttered under my breath that no one in their right mind would admit to being found guilty of anything if they wanted to get a PI license, Stella rolled her eyes and tapped the page for me to finish.

I returned the mountain of paper to the crabby crone, who told me to resume my seat, and that the examiner would be with me shortly.

That was at 10 a.m. By 1 p.m., we were still waiting.

For the tenth time, I inquired when we would be seen.

For the tenth time, she replied, "When he is ready."

She did not take kindly to this office being compared with the speed and efficiency of the Department of Motor Vehicles. We were on the verge of coming to blows when a spindly man with a pointed nose and glasses appeared from a side office.

"Mr. Butterfield? Mr. Jacob Butterfield?"

Ignoring the receptionist, I smiled broadly at the man. "Right here, sir."

"This way please." He stepped to one side, allowing me to precede him into the office.

"May my office manager join us?" I indicated Stella.

"It's a little unusual, but I don't see why not."

Escorting Stella into the office, I noted the name on the door: John Watson.

If ever there was a man born to handle detectives.

John Watson's inner sanctum revealed a wealth of knowledge about the man. Where most would have pictures of scenery, wildlife or, at least, some family photographs, the walls were adorned with images of famous authors, of the detective variety no less.

A portrait of Sir Arthur Canon Doyle, leaning against a chair back, his mustache properly waxed in true Edwardian style. Next to him, the most famous female author of the genre, Agatha Christie.

Two Americans, who, I admit, were my personal favorites also earned a place on his wall, Raymond Chandler of the detective Philip Marlowe fame, and the father of hard-boiled detectives, the former Pinkerton agent, Dashiell Hammett.

Watson's neatly arranged bookshelves sported their many novels, as well as several other authors unfamiliar to me. The Library of Congress would have been jealous of his collection. I could not stop myself from admiring them up close.

Watson joined me. "I may not possess any discernible writing skills, but I like to think I create my own detectives as well." He smiled beatifically, adding, "Let's get on with this, shall we?"

At Watson's invitation, I sat next to Stella, while he settled into the capacious chair behind his desk and thumbed through the paperwork, his rapidity attesting to the frequency with which he performed this ritual. Periodically, he paused to inspect an answer, taking a pencil from a cup to circle it.

I questioned whether I was standing in front of St Peter while my life errors were reviewed, with a favorable verdict being in serious doubt.

After what felt like an eternity, he put down his pencil.

"All seems to be in order, but I do have a few questions. First, with a distinguished career as a San Francisco police detective, serving in both Vice and Homicide, something I'm sure even the great Sam Spade..." he glanced up at Hammett,

Spade's author, "...would find confusing, why leave so quickly?"

Shit, I thought. *What can I say to convince him?*

"Well, sir…" smoothly, Stella intervened to save my bacon before I could make a fool of myself, "I take responsibility for that. I grew wary of the night I would receive a knock at the door and two officers on the threshold telling me something had happened to my Jacob."

The sincerity in her voice caught me off guard, and I stared at her, momentarily nonplussed.

"Which begs the question, ma'am, why on earth allow him to get a PI license? Does that not involve the same risks?" Watson pressed reasonably.

"Perhaps, but this way he can pick and choose, and not simply be assigned. Besides, look at him, do you think he could shed the police life completely for little ol' me? To you, it might seem like a curious compromise but, to me, it is mutually beneficial, and the lesser evil."

I felt sweat bead across my brow at Watson's scrutiny, but he did not appear to notice.

"Fair enough, I can accept that," he conceded. "I assume you are willing to vouch for his personal integrity, miss?"

I nearly choked at the question. *If anyone has a checkered past, it is the woman corroborating mine.*

"Assuredly, I am, sir." She nodded graciously. "If you call this number, and ask to speak with Lieutenant Louis Mazzetti, Jacob's former partner…" my knees buckled at the suggestion, "…he will verify Jacob's professional prowess. Make sure to tell him Stella Fitzhugh gave you his number."

Watson inclined his head. "If you two will step out to the waiting room, I will be a moment."

Doing as instructed, I leaned close to Stella to whisper angrily, "Are you insane? Mazzetti is the one who caused all this. He is more likely to ensure I am permanently in the unemployment line, than affirm my good standing."

Stella patted my arm then hooked hers through it. "Have faith, my love. You'll see."

We sat in the hard chairs listening to the clack of the typewriters, their bells chiming cheerfully at the end of each line.

Watson appeared at his door and waved us in. "Lieutenant Mazzetti was very forthcoming and confessed he was disappointed by your sudden retirement. Apparently, you will be missed by the department."

Seeing the light at the end of the tunnel, I elected not to spit at the word *retirement*.

The examiner continued, "Normally, we require you to wait until we make our determination, however, I see no reason to delay the formalities."

I accepted his extended hand with a smile, and we shook.

"Allow me to congratulate you, Mr. Butterfield on becoming the newest Private Investigator in California," he declared.

He produced a form from his desk drawer. "As it takes several weeks for your official license and identification to be dispatched, you can use this temporary certificate."

Bidding him farewell, we left. It had been a long day including all those hours of tedious waiting, and we were famished, so stopped at a diner on the way back to the motor lodge where, I observed, "You really do have Lou dangling on your strings."

Stella's smile was nothing short of triumphant. "Let's just say he will dance to our command."

POSTSCRIPT

A busy Wednesday morning resulted in a blank canvas being turned into an office worthy of the title *Jacob Butterfield: Private Investigator*. The early morning sunlight flickering through the beautiful stained-glass window composed myriad rainbows on every surface.

Somehow, Stella had negotiated the use of the landlord's crew to transfer the furniture from storage, after she received written notification we would *not* be sharing the place with mice.

The screech of wooden legs being dragged across the polished floor as each piece was arranged to Stella's satisfaction, drowned out the entrance of one Lieutenant Louis Mazzetti.

He strolled through the open door, careful his ox of a body did not jar the signwriter, who was taking great pains not to screw up my name.

Seeing the colored light bathing the office elicited a wisecrack from my former partner, "You running a church in here or something, Jake?"

"Hah! If I was, you'd have been struck down before you made it across the threshold."

"Very funny," Lou shot back. There was a loaded pause as though he was weighing something up, then he added casually, "Thought you might like to know, the Feds connected Mae and June's deaths to the two murders in Chinatown, along with another couple of bodies found in similar circumstances."

He didn't elaborate, but I felt vindicated, and could not prevent a small grin of triumph.

Before I could respond, Stella appeared, greeting Lou with a curt nod. "Lieutenant."

"Miss Fitzhugh." Lou tipped his hat. "Oh, and Miss Fitzhugh, I am a busy man. Do not think you can send every Tom, Dick, and Harry to me to vouch for this place."

Stella's grin was unrepentant. "Fair enough, I guess they could go to that Internal Affairs guy instead. What was his name again?"

Mazzetti blanched. "You best hope you never need a cop in the middle of the night." He flexed his muscles… as though *that* would intimidate Stella.

"Already have one in my bed, and another at my beck and call. Why would I need more?"

Flushing in agitation, he marched out of the office, bumping into the painter who dropped his jar of paint.

The artist frowned. "I'm out of paint, Mr. Butterfield. I'll have to order more, but I'll finish as quickly as possible."

I glanced at the glass panel in the door and shook my head.

Go figure.

If you are ever in the Mission District of San Francisco and require the services of an excellent and highly recommended private investigator, make sure to check out the office of one *Jacob Butter.*

DERELICTION OF DEVOTION

Butters P.I.

CHAPTER ONE

1940 - San Francisco

The funny thing about life is you never know what fate has in store. Case in point, the opening of yours truly's private investigations office at the onset of the Second World War.

It's one thing for the average schmuck to hang a shingle and call himself a gumshoe, but when a disgraced member of the San Francisco Homicide Squad does it, the shadiest of clientele crawl out of the woodwork and there is no lack of them in the City by the Bay.

Friday September 13th, 1940, started out pretty much like any other day... in the midst of a worldwide strife. Buckingham Palace, King George VI's London home was damaged by German bombs during the air raids known as the Blitz.

In Africa, Italian troops under Marshal Graziani attacked Egypt in an effort to drive the British out.

In my little corner of the world, Friday the 13th marked a significant, and unlucky, turning point in my life.

It all began with my business partner, and live-in lover,

Stella Fitzhugh, reviewing the files. From the moment we offered our... well, mine mostly... services to the city, our caseload was unrelenting.

Cheating spouses, missing people, minor thefts and suchlike, along with any and all offences the various police departments deemed unworthy of investigation, were dropped at our doorstep. All had to be solved and invoiced.

Especially since we had bills to pay.

On this particular morning, I was following some slime-ball around the city who was bedding any woman naive enough to fall for his BS about being widowed, while his stay-at-home wife nursed a baby bottle of scotch and paid twenty-five dollars a day plus expenses to collect evidence for the express purpose of saving her marriage.

I may judge people's motivation for hiring us but, as long as their checks clear, I don't judge them... much.

The problem with this case was the amount of time it was taking me out of the office, leaving me less time with my bedmate.

...but I digress...

Whoever said peeping through keyholes for a living... figuratively speaking, of course... wasn't arduous, never spent any time as a private investigator with a client who demanded immediate proof that her husband was cheating.

Exhausted, I dragged myself back to the office around ten in the evening, surprised to see Stella's silhouette through the frosted glass of the door.

I turned the knob to find it locked, relieved that, even if she knows I'm on my way, she has the foresight to consider her safety when alone in the office — especially at night.

Digging out my keys, I unlocked the door and went in to find Stella staring at the entrance blankly. She was unnervingly still.

Concerned, I crossed the floor.

As though the sound of my approach broke a spell, she refocused, and folded her arms, barking, "Take one more step, Jacob Butterfield, and I'll give you a demonstration of the fancy nickel-plated pistol you bought me out of petty cash and how much better my aim has become since you shelled out for shooting lessons."

"How very generous of me." I grinned, trying to break whatever tension had suddenly filled the office... and our relationship.

"Don't waste your breath humoring me. Just park your butt in that chair." She jabbed a finger at the one across from her desk.

My smile faded and I felt like a schoolboy being hauled in front of the principal for a misdemeanor I failed to recall.

"We need to talk," she said flatly. "Are you done with the cheating husband case, or do you need more time to comfort the poor distraught wife, while getting your jollies watching the man diddle his secretary?" adding, facetiously, "or have you decided to join in the fun?"

My forehead puckered into an uncomprehending frown. Stella knew I did not play around. I had hardly looked at another woman since our loose friendship... which, occasionally included sex... had evolved into whatever this was.

"Stella, I don't know what you're talking about but, rest assured, everything will be wrapped up in the next day—"

"Wrong, Butterfield, you close that case tonight. Have a courier deliver the evidence, along with our final bill. If that doesn't satisfy her, she can sue us."

"I know Eleanor—"

"Eleanor? Oh, we are on a first name basis with the client?" her voice dripped with sarcasm.

"No," I corrected the slip. "Mrs. Peterson had additional information concerning where and when I could find her husband."

"How much more does she need? Surely, given how *diligently* you have worked," I heard the snarky emphasis on diligently and my brow creased at her allusion, "she has enough evidence to win twenty divorce cases. This has gone way beyond what she hired us to do."

"Why the fit of the grumps, Stella? It's not like Rich Aunt Moneybags..." hopefully a certain board game company will forgive me for the feminization of their famed wealthy uncle in an attempt to diffuse the friction, "...hasn't missed a payment as she?"

Annoyed, she countered, "No, but we have other cases that need your..." she amended, "...*our* attention."

She picked up a file and pushed it over the desk to me. A picture of an odd-looking diamond, torn from a book, slid out along with handwritten notes about its original discovery centuries ago, and its loss from a Flemish chateau during the last war.

"Looks like someone spent the day at the library," I teased lightly.

"For the money we are looking at for recovering that rock, you bet."

"How much?" I asked idly. Her reply prompted a shocked, "Twenty-thousand dollars? Stella, who has that kind of dough? I take it this prospective client is not some minor royal fleeing a revolution?"

"Not that I'm aware."

"Then who?" I stared at her.

A faint blush washed up her cheeks. "I don't know. His

representative was tight lipped in that regard, but come on Jacob, we could use the money," she argued diffidently.

I couldn't refute that, and tried to keep an open mind, while unpleasant possibilities chased through my head.

Reading the paperwork, one detail nagged at me. "Recover? Says here, the diamond vanished at the end of the Great War, probably appropriated by a returning soldier, and hasn't been seen since."

"Let's just say, news of its loss is a little premature. Seems someone here in the States was able to acquire it."

"The non-royal," I said sarcastically, "who is willing to pay a handsome fee for finding an already found rock? Any chance it's the previous owners, assuming they are still alive?"

"I have no clue what happened to them," Stella huffed. "Have you even read my notes? It's the guy who bought it five or six years ago, but he doesn't want to be kept hanging until your adolescent infatuation with a millionaire's wife comes to an end."

Ignoring Stella's appraisal of my business concerns with Eleanor Peterson, I returned to the matter at hand. "Let me get this straight. The guy who bought a stolen diamond wants us to recover it. From whom?"

"The thief."

It was all I could do not to roll my eyes and slap my forehead.

"Okay, Stella, how about we start this conversation over again."

RORI BLEU

With a smattering of riverboat pirates and royalty in her
heritage, Rori Bleu's childhood reflected her past.
An interest in fairy tales, myth and legend were as important
as spirited discussions around politics and current affairs —
although some might argue they are one and the same!

A fascination, sparked by listening to Grimm's Fairy Tales at
her grandmother's knee, not only encouraged Rori's passion
for reading, but also steered her into the world of RPG's.
What began as a fun pastime, soon evolved into the creation
of fantastical worlds, but Rori never lost her love of politics
going on to specialise in Governmental History and
Historical Research.

Naturally this means her stories are steeped in historical
accuracy and real-life intrigue. While Rori's love of a happily
ever after means her preferred genre is romance, don't be
surprised if you discover an occasional detour into historical
fiction, thrillers, horror and fantasy.

ROSIE CHAPEL

Rosie Chapel lives in Perth, Australia, with her hubby and two rescue fur babies. When not writing, she loves catching up with friends, burying herself in a book (or three), discovering the wonders of Western Australia, or — and the best — a quiet evening at home with her husband, enjoying a glass of wine and a movie.

Website: www.rosiechapel.com

ALSO BY RORI BLEU

Pineapple Meringue

Imprisoned Hearts

Port of London

Dani's Masquerade

Black Tulips

Ajei's Destiny

Porta Aeternum

The Queen's Heart

Syn *with Matthew Forester*

With Rosie Chapel

Tapestry of Shadows and Light - The Hunters Prequel

Echoes and Illusions - The Hunters: Book 1

Smoke and Mirrors - The Hunters : Book 2

Evie's War

Vindicta

Corrupt Covenant

Lesser of Two Evils

Deadly Incision

Tidbits

The Sela Helsdatter Saga

A Flip of The Coin - Book One

Conceived Chaos - Book Two

Odin's Bane - Book Three

Valhalla's Doom - Book Four

Arcane Alchemy: Freya's Fate - *A Helsdatter Saga Novella*

Butters PI

Double Cross

Dereliction of Devotion

Sibling Rivalry

The Mobster's Moll

ALSO BY ROSIE CHAPEL

<u>Historical Fiction</u>

The Hannah's Heirloom Sequence
The Pomegranate Tree - Book One
Echoes of Stone and Fire - Book Two
Embers of Destiny - Book Three
Etched in Starlight - Prequel
Hannah's Heirloom Trilogy - Compilation — e-book only

Prelude to Fate
Legacy of Flame and Ash

The Nettleby Trilogy (WW1 Novellas)
A Guardian Unexpected - Book One
Under the Clock - Book Two
Between Heartbeats - Book Three

<u>Regency Romances</u>
The Linen and Lace Series
Once Upon An Earl - Book One
To Unlock Her Heart - Book Two
Love on a Winter's Tide - Book Three
A Love Unquenchable - Book Four
A Hidden Rose — Book Five

An Unexpected Romance
Elusive Hearts - Book One

Shrouded Hearts - Book Two

The Daffodil Garden

The Unconventional Duchess

Rescuing Her Knight - *the de Wiltons:* Book One

His Fiery Hoyden

A Regency Duet

A Regency Christmas Double

Fate is Curious

A Christmas Prayer *with Ashlee Shades*

The Lady's Wager

Winning Emma

A Love Impossible

Unravelling Roana

Love Kindled

Moonbeams and Mistletoe

The Baron's Inheritance

<u>Fairy Tale Romance</u>

Chasing Bluebells

<u>Contemporary Romances</u>

Of Ruins and Romance

All At Once It's You

Cobweb Dreams

Just One Step

His Heart's Second Sigh

With Rori Bleu

Tapestry of Shadows and Light - The Hunters Prequel

Echoes and Illusions - The Hunters: Book 1

Smoke and Mirrors - The Hunters : Book 2

Evie's War

Vindicta

Corrupt Covenant

Lesser of Two Evils

Deadly Incision

Tidbits

The Sela Helsdatter Saga

A Flip of The Coin - Book One

Conceived Chaos - Book Two

Odin's Bane - Book Three

Valhalla's Doom - Book Four

Arcane Alchemy: Freya's Fate - *A Helsdatter Saga Novella*

Butters PI

Double Cross

Dereliction of Devotion

Sibling Rivalry

The Mobster's Moll

www.ingramcontent.com/pod-product-compliance
Lightning Source LLC
Chambersburg PA
CBHW072145180726
48291CB00005BA/1702